Wrong Way Around Magic

written and illustrated by Ruth Chew

cover illustrated by Rudy Nappi

A
LITTLE APPLE
PAPERBACK

SCHOLASTIC INC.

New York   Toronto   London   Auckland   Sydney

To my grandson
Liam S. McGrail

No part of this publication may be reproduced in whole or in part, or
stored in a retrieval system, or transmitted in any form or by any
means, electronic, mechanical, photocopying, recording, or
otherwise, without written permission of the publisher.
For information regarding permission, write to Scholastic Inc.,
730 Broadway, New York, NY 10003.

ISBN 0-590-46023-4

12 11 10 9 8 7 6 5 4 3 2 1   3 4 5 6 7 8/9

Printed in the U.S.A.   40

First Scholastic printing, January 1993

Wrong Way Around Magic

1

"WILLY," Mrs. Gerston said to her daughter. "We'll have supper as soon as your dad has finished watching the ball game on television. So stay close to home."

She turned to her son. "Remember, Chip, I don't want to have to hunt for either of you. Please try not to get lost!"

Chip and Wilma went upstairs to the spare room that was full of things that there was no space for anywhere else in the house.

Chip picked up an old pair of field glasses from the cluttered top of a chest of drawers. "I never saw these before. I wonder where they came from?" He handed his sister the glasses.

"The paint is wearing off, and the rim is missing from one lens," Wilma said. "Someone has tied a shoelace to them. I guess that's so you can hang them around your neck."

She looked through the field glasses at a little brown bird on the telephone wire outside the window. Now she could see that the bird had a rosy neck and face. He seemed so close, Wilma felt that she could reach out and stroke his soft feathers. "They work okay." Wilma handed the field glasses to her brother.

Chip pointed them at the neighbor's back yard. "There's Jimmy Murphy. He still has egg on his face from breakfast!"

Wilma sat on the sofa that could be changed into a bed whenever the Gerstons had an overnight guest. She looked at the strange painting hanging on the wall across the room. It showed twisted trees clinging to tall rocky islands that seemed to float on misty lakes. Wilma never tired of looking at it.

Chip sat down beside his sister and turned the field glasses back to front. The big lenses were so far apart that he could only see through one of them. He stared through the glass at the picture. "Hey, Willy, this makes everything tiny!"

Wilma looked through the other large lens. At first the picture seemed far away. Then it came closer until it filled the circle of light in front of her. Suddenly the light began to move away again. At last it became so faint that Wilma could hardly see it at all.

She stood up and turned around. There was no light behind her, and the sofa had disappeared. She seemed to be in a dark tunnel.

Wilma felt cold all over. She couldn't see Chip anywhere.

Her brother was two years younger than she was, and her mother had told Wilma that she had to watch out for him. But right now she really wanted Chip for company. Magic always seemed such fun in books. But this was just plain scary.

2

"CHIP!" Wilma called as loud as she could. Her voice echoed in the shadowy tunnel.

She heard a faint answer. "Willy! Where are you?"

Her eyes were getting used to the darkness. Up ahead she could see a dim light. Wilma started to run toward it. The tunnel seemed to go on forever. She was out of breath by the time she came to the end.

She had to climb down from the tunnel to reach the ground.

Wilma looked back and saw another tunnel next to the one she had just left. Both tunnels were set in the wall of a large black building.

Someone jumped out of the second tunnel and landed near her.

It was Chip!

"Willy," he said, "what happened?"

Wilma was so glad to see her brother that for a moment she couldn't speak. She pointed to the two tunnels.

Now they were covered with curved glass doors. One door had a rim around it. Both doors seemed to be shrinking. So was the black building.

The next thing they knew, the field glasses were on the ground at their feet.

"At least now we know they're magic!" Chip picked up the glasses.

"Aren't you afraid to touch them, Chip?" Wilma said. "We don't know what they'll do next."

Chip thought about this. "I'm not sure what they've done *now*."

Chip and Wilma were standing on a rocky ledge overlooking a large lake. In the distance they could see mountains rising out of the mist.

A little house was built on the ledge. The house was just a straw roof held up by four posts.

"There's a house like that in the picture we were looking at," Chip said.

For a moment Wilma didn't say anything. Then she whispered, "Chip, somehow we've got ourselves into that picture!"

"That's neat, Willy!" Chip said. "This place looks like fun to explore."

"Mom was almost ready to serve supper. And she told us not to get lost," Wilma reminded him. "We can come back here another time. Right now we'd better go home."

"Here goes!" Chip turned the field glasses around and looked through one of the large lenses. Wilma stood beside him and looked through the other.

Now the little house with the straw roof seemed very far away. But nothing magic happened. Chip and Wilma were still on the ledge over the lake.

Chip tried staring through the small lenses. The field glasses only made the straw-roofed house look much nearer.

"We're stuck here! I guess I made a big mistake fooling with these things. How was I to know they were magic?" Chip handed the glasses to his sister.

Wilma was frightened, but she didn't want her brother to know it. She looked through the glasses. "Chip, there's someone in that house!"

3

CHIP looked through the field glasses. "You're right, Willy. There *is* somebody in there! Let's go see who it is." He handed his sister the glasses and started walking toward the little house.

Wilma hung the field glasses around her neck and started after her brother.

Because the house had no walls, they could see someone seated at a small table there. When they came closer they saw that it was a boy of about fourteen. He was writing on a sheet of paper with a pointed brush. He didn't notice Wilma and Chip even when they came right up to the house.

They stood just outside the shadow of the straw roof and waited for the boy to look up. He kept on working.

At last Chip said, "Hello!"

The boy put down his brush and stood

up. He smiled and bowed to the two children. "Greetings," he said. "Forgive my rudeness. I did not know you were here."

"What are you writing?" Wilma asked.

"A poem," the boy told her.

"I love poetry! Tell it to us, please!" Wilma begged.

The boy smiled and recited, "The soft white mist reaches the knees of the mountain. Soon the evening shadows will fall. I must go home before I am lost in the dark."

He looked out at the lake. "I'm afraid I'll forget it if I don't get it all written down. Please excuse me while I write. Then I can talk to you. You can sit here." He pointed to a bench in the little summer house.

Chip and Wilma waited until the boy had finished writing. Then he said, "My name is Ying. What is yours?"

"I'm Chip, and Willy is my sister."

"This is a lonely place," Ying said. "I didn't know anyone lived near here. It's not safe after dark. You ought to go home soon."

"We want to go home," Chip told him, "but we don't know how. We were brought here by magic."

"I am a scholar, and I do not believe in magic," Ying said.

Wilma stood up. "We didn't believe in it, either — until today."

Ying looked hard at her. "Tell me what happened."

Together Wilma and Chip told him how the field glasses had brought them into the painting. Ying reached for the glasses. Wilma handed them to him.

He looked at something far away across the lake. "I can see the rooftops of our village from here."

Ying turned the glasses back to front

and stared through one of the big lenses.
"Now everything seems far away." He
gave the glasses back. "They're a clever
toy, but if they were magic, I could go
home the way you came here."

"We tried to make the glasses take us
back," Chip told him. "But I guess we're
stuck here."

"Magic or no magic," Ying said, "you'd
better come home with me."

4

YING walked away from the little summer house. He stepped off the ledge onto a narrow path that led down the cliff. Chip and Wilma followed him.

The path went around huge rocks and over soft crumbly pebbles. Ying showed Wilma and Chip how to keep from falling by grabbing hold of the rough grass and twisted trees that grew between the stones.

At last they came to the lake at the foot of the cliff. They made their way along the jagged shore to a long, thin point of rocks that stretched out into the water.

Ying pointed to an arched stone bridge at the end of the point. "Hurry! We have to get across that before dark." He began to run toward the bridge.

The narrow strip of land was like a long causeway. Wilma and Chip picked their way carefully among the sharp stones. A cold damp fog was rising from the lake on both sides of them. They could hear water lapping against the stones near their feet. But the fog was so thick that they couldn't see the water.

Ying was waiting for them at the bridge. It arched up out of the fog, but the fog was still rising. And there were no railings on the bridge.

"You go first, Willy," Ying said. "Chip must follow you. I will come last to see that you get safely across. The water is deep in this spot."

Wilma started up the curve of the bridge. She planted each foot carefully

on the damp stone, marched across the top and down the other side. Finally she stepped off the bridge onto a patch of soft marshy ground with slender trees growing on it.

Chip and Ying were close behind Wilma. Ying led the way through the grove of trees. They came again to the lake.

Wilma looked around. "I thought we'd reached the other side of the lake, but this is just a little island."

"Yes," Ying told her. "But the lake is shallow on this side of it."

Ying rolled his baggy pants high over his knees. He took off his sandals and carried them. Then he waded into the water.

Chip and Wilma hung their sneakers around their necks. Wilma's sneakers hung down, one on each side of the field glasses.

They waded after Ying through dense weeds that grew in the lake. In a very short time they stepped out on another shore. By now the sun was going down.

As soon as they all had their shoes on and their pants legs rolled down, Ying led the way through a patch of scraggly trees up to the top of a hill.

In the gloom they could just make out the shapes of houses. They couldn't see any lights. "Come," Ying said, "I want you to meet my family."

5

THERE were about twelve houses in a clearing on top of the hill. They had tile roofs and walls of sun-baked bricks. The houses were built close to each other and all looked alike.

Each house had two doors facing the street. The door on the left was the larger one.

Ying ran to bang on the large door of one of the houses. "It's me, Ying!"

There were no windows on this side of the house, but Wilma and Chip thought there must be a peephole. They heard someone say, "Who is with you?"

"Two children from a far country," Ying answered. "They are lost and do not know how to return home. I could not leave them alone at night on Crag Island."

There was no answer from inside the house.

Ying spoke again. "Please let these children come in. They are not older than my sister and brother. If Mee and Heing were lost in a strange land, would you like them to be left outdoors in the dark?"

There was a long wait. Wilma thought she heard whispering from the other side of the door. Then there was the sound of the door being unbarred. It was opened by a man who seemed frightened of something.

"This is Chip. Willy is his sister," Ying said. "And this," he told the children, "is my father. He is called Chun."

Ying's father bowed to the children and held the door open just wide enough for them to go in one at a time.

When they were all inside the house, Chun barred the door with a thick slab of wood. Then Ying introduced his mother, Tang. Wilma thought something was worrying her, but Tang smiled and welcomed them.

They met Ying's brother, Heing, who was a little older than Chip, and his sister, Mee, who was about the same age as Wilma.

They don't want us here, Wilma thought, but they're being nice about it.

She looked around. The room seemed to be a kitchen. Bunches of herbs and roots hung from the ceiling along with hunks of meat that were being dried for future use.

By the light of the burning wick in a

dish of oil, Tang began to cut up vegetables with a cleaver. Her chopping
board was a thick piece of tree trunk.

A big brick stove faced the street door.
Behind the stove was a pile of dry grass
and husks.

Wilma saw that Mee was using some
of the grass to make a fire under a black
iron bowl on the stove. She went over
to help.

6

It took an hour for the iron bowl to become hot enough to cook the vegetables. A dish of rice was set to steam on the stove in a pan of water with a lid on it.

When the rice was ready, Tang put the vegetables and some gingerroot into the iron bowl and quickly cooked them. Mee filled seven bowls with rice, and Wilma put them on the table. Next Mee set out a pitcher of boiled water. Then she handed Wilma fourteen smooth sticks with flat sides.

"Are these what you eat with?" Wilma asked.

"Of course," Mee told her. "In your country, do people eat everything with their fingers?"

"We use knives and forks and spoons," Wilma told her.

Mee picked up a little china scoop. "Here's a spoon," she said. "Knives are for cooking. What's a fork?"

Chip had been telling Chun about the magic field glasses while Ying and his brother listened. The glasses were still around Wilma's neck. Everybody wanted to look at them.

Tang put a big platter of vegetables in the middle of the table. "Eat now and play with the glasses later," she said.

They sat on small wooden benches. Mee showed Wilma how to use the eating sticks like tongs.

Wilma learned to raise the bowl to her mouth with her left hand and use the sticks in her right hand to move the rice into her mouth.

Tang turned her own sticks around. She used the ends she had not had in her mouth to pick up delicious vegetables from the platter. Tang put them in Wilma's bowl on top of the rice.

Ying showed Chip how to use the sticks. It was some time before he finally managed to get a mouthful of rice. Then everybody at the table put down their sticks and clapped their hands.

Chip grinned as Chun began to load his rice bowl with vegetables.

When all the bowls were empty, Heing filled them with warm water from the pitcher on the table. They drank every drop.

Chun stood up to show that the meal was over.

"Thank you for the delicious supper," Wilma said.

"I don't usually like vegetables, Tang," Chip admitted. "I wish my mother could cook them to taste like that."

Tang smiled.

But deep inside her Wilma felt guilty. She could see that Ying and his family had only just enough to eat. They had less because they'd shared their food with her and Chip.

7

WILMA helped Mee and Tang clear the table and wash the dishes. Ying and Chip were busy showing Ying's father and brother the field glasses.

"Ying often goes to Crag Island so he can have a quiet place to study," Tang said. "It is very hard to learn to read and write, but Ying loves the work."

"I like to read, too," Wilma told her. "And I'm getting better at writing."

"Who taught you?" Mee asked.

"I learned in school," Wilma answered.

"Only boys go to school here," Tang said. "Not many are able to learn. Chun can only read a little bit, and he can hardly write at all. Heing works hard at his lessons, but he doesn't enjoy them as Ying did at his age. We are proud that Ying is doing so well. In our country, scholars are the most important people."

When the dishes were all put away, Chun and the boys walked over to the wooden table.

Chip gave Wilma the field glasses. She hung them around her neck.

Tang picked up the dish of oil with the burning wick floating in it. "Bedtime!" She opened a door in the back wall of the kitchen.

Ying bowed to Chip and Wilma. "Come into our bedroom."

Tang led the way, and everybody followed her. Chun came last. He shut the bedroom door behind him.

There were two large bamboo beds. Each had curtains of mosquito netting around it. There were no mattresses or

sheets or blankets, only bamboo slats to
sleep on.

Chun laid a stick of pressed powder
on the clay floor between the beds. He
took the lamp and lit one end of the stick.
It glowed red and began to smoke and
give off a strange smell.

"What's that for?" Chip asked.

"To keep away mosquitoes," Ying told
him.

Chun handed the lamp to Ying. Then he and Tang took off their sandals and climbed into one of the beds. They lay down in the clothes they were wearing and pulled the curtains of netting around them.

Then all five young people kicked off their sneakers or sandals and climbed into the other bed.

Chip was on one side of Wilma, and Mee was on the other. "Sleep well," Mee said softly in her ear.

Soon, everyone but Wilma and Chip was sleeping.

"Willy," Chip whispered. "We can't stay here. How are we going to get home?"

"I don't know," Wilma said, "but as long as we have the field glasses, we're sure to be all right."

8

NEXT morning, as soon as it was light, all the children in the big wooden bed sat up and stretched. Tang and Chun were already up. Their bed was empty.

Wilma and Chip slipped from under the net curtains and climbed out of bed.

Mee was putting on her sandals. "I like to wash my face in the morning."

"So do I," Wilma told her. "But Chip wouldn't mind if he never got washed."

"You and I will go to the well, Willy," Mee told her.

"I'll go, too," Chip said. "I'm not great on washing, but I'd like a drink of cold water."

Ying was out of bed now. "We always boil water before we drink it, Chip. I'll get you a drink if you're thirsty."

"We have to show our guests our living room," Heing reminded his brother.

Ying opened a different door from the one they'd used to come into the bedroom. He led the way into a room much bigger than the kitchen or the bedroom. When everybody had come in, Ying closed the door tightly behind them.

This room was brighter than the others. The center of the roof was open to

the sky. In one corner Chun was feeding
dry grass to a large animal with horns.

"That's a water buffalo," Chip told
Wilma. "I saw one on television."

In another corner a mother pig nursed
a lot of little pigs. A rooster perched on
the handle of a plow. Four hens watched
over chicks of various ages. Another hen
sat on a nest behind a stack of spades
and hoes.

A large table and a number of wooden seats with no backs were set up near a door. When the door opened, Tang came out of the kitchen. She put a large pot of steaming rice porridge on the table.

Mee ran to get bowls and the little china scoops she called spoons.

Ying brought a pitcher and poured some water into one of the bowls. "How's this, Chip?"

"Thank you." Chip drank the water.

Then Tang filled the bowls with porridge. Everybody sat down to eat. Wilma and Chip were very hungry.

As soon as his bowl was empty, Heing told Wilma and Chip, "I have to go to school now." From a shelf he took a book with wooden boards for covers, a roll of paper, and a pointed brush. Then he opened a small door that led to the street.

Mee picked up two jugs. She handed one to Wilma. "Come on!"

The two girls went out of the door after Heing. He began running toward a small building halfway down the little street. Mee pointed to it. "That's the schoolhouse."

Wilma heard the sound of boys' voices chanting. "What are they singing?" she asked.

"They're reciting what they've been reading," Mee told her. "They have to know it by heart. Ying doesn't go to school here now. He already knows more than the teacher, so he studies his books by himself."

9

THE well was across the little street from
the schoolhouse.

"We're in luck," Mee said. "No one is
ahead of us." She reached up to grab a
long bamboo pole that tilted up from the
well.

Wilma was taller than Mee. She stood
on tiptoe and took hold of the highest

part of the pole she could reach. Together the girls yanked the end of the
pole down.

This raised the other end of the pole,
which had a rope tied to it. A bucket tied
to the rope was pulled up.

Wilma held onto the bamboo pole,
while Mee lifted the bucket of water out
of the well.

The girls filled their jugs and then
splashed the remaining water on their
faces. The cool water felt wonderful.

A young woman arrived with two pails
hanging from a pole over one shoulder.

Mee ran to set down the pails. "Toy,"
she said. "I want you to meet Willy. She
is a traveler from far away who is staying
at our house."

The woman looked frightened. She
bowed to Wilma, but she didn't smile.

Wilma remembered that Chun
seemed frightened at first when he had

opened his door to let her and Chip come in the night before.

The girls helped Toy fill her pails with water. She thanked them and carried the pails away.

"My mother will be wondering what happened to us." Mee picked up her jug of water and started for home. Wilma followed right behind.

Tang was waiting at the kitchen door. She took the jugs of water. "Sh-sh! Ying is working in the living room. Why don't you go and help in the gardens? Chip is there with Chun." Tang handed each girl a basket.

Wilma looked around for the gardens. She expected them to be behind the house.

Instead, Mee led her back down the street, past the schoolhouse, the well, and all the other houses.

The street became a narrow path between small fields cut into the side of the hill like steps.

People were working here. Some of the fields were flooded. Much to her surprise, Wilma saw her brother standing knee-deep in water. He was holding a net, trying to scoop something from between the stems of the plants.

"What are you doing, Chip?" Wilma asked.

Chip looked up and grinned. "Fishing," he said.

10

"Got one!" Chip held up his net. A shiny fish was flopping around in it.

Chun was working in the next little field, which was higher on the hill. When he heard Chip, he pulled a pail from a load of things on the back of the water buffalo. Chun brought the pail to the edge of the flooded field. "Put any fish you catch in this, Chip," he said. Then he went back to work.

Chip waded over and dumped the fish into the pail. He caught sight of another fish swimming between the stalks of grain. Chip moved quietly toward it, holding the net ready.

"We'd better not stay here," Mee whispered. "We'll scare the fish."

"How did the fish get in the field?" Wilma asked.

"We put little baby ones there when we planted the rice." Mee led the way up the hill to a row of trees next to the field where Chun was working.

Wilma saw that there was fruit on the trees. The pears were still hard and green. A few peaches were ripe. And both plum trees had red and yellow fruit on them.

"Oh, dear!" Mee pointed to some plums on the ground. "We'd better hurry before any more are spoiled."

Wilma went over to the peach tree. "I'm going to pick the ripe ones before the birds get to them."

Both girls worked steadily. When Wilma had picked all the ripe peaches she could reach, she went to help Mee with the plums.

It was a hot day. The sun beat down

upon their heads. They were glad when Chun came to tell them it was mealtime. He roped the heavy baskets of fruit onto the water buffalo. It was already carrying the tools. The pail of water now had four live fish flopping around in it. Somehow Chun managed to load the pail and the fish onto the animal's back, too.

They walked single file along the narrow path that led to the village. When they passed the schoolhouse, the door opened and about fifteen boys of different ages came out.

Heing ran to join Chip. "You're lucky!" he said when Chip showed him the fish. "I never get a chance to go fishing. I'm always in school."

"What about after school and weekends?" Chip asked.

Heing had never heard of weekends. He said he went to school until the evening meal and had homework after that. "Yesterday was different," he said. "We ate very late because Ying had not come home. I did my homework while we waited for him."

11

TANG cut the fish into small pieces and cooked them with the vegetables Chung had brought from his field. They all enjoyed them with their rice.

After the meal Heing went back to school. Ying sat down with his books. And Chip and Chun took the water buffalo back to work in the field.

Tang handed a sickle to her daughter, and a pole pointed on both ends to Wilma.

"We're going to cut fuel," Mee told Wilma.

The two girls went out of the door into the village street.

Wilma looked around and saw a big door and a smaller one on each house. "Mee," she said, "why are the houses exactly alike?"

"This is the way we build houses in our village," Mee told her. "To do anything different would bring bad luck to everyone here. Something terrible could happen if anything is changed."

The girls walked through the village and past the little fields cut into the sides of the hills. They followed a steep narrow path that led up the side of one of the hills. The ground here was too stony for crops to be planted, but weeds and wild grass were sprouting between the stones.

"Someone else has found my secret fuel patch, Willy!" Mee pointed to where the weeds had been chopped off close to the ground. "We won't be able to cook our food if we can't find fuel."

"Grass burns too quickly," Wilma said. "Why don't you use wood instead?"

"We don't have enough wood left around here to burn it up. Grass grows faster." Mee cut every weed and blade of grass that was left and gave them to Wilma to carry. The two climbed higher.

Now Wilma could see out over the lake and past the islands to the misty mountains. She saw that most of what was green had been cut, and the hills were brown and bare. She was carrying the pole Tang had given her and a small bunch of weeds.

Suddenly Mee caught sight of the field glasses hanging around Wilma's neck. "Willy, hand me your magic toy."

Wilma gave her the glasses. Mee

looked through them at the high hill
overhead. "Willy, I see something
green!"

Mee handed back the glasses, and the
girls started to climb. They found a deep
ditch filled with grass. Mee cut every bit
and made two huge tangled bundles.

Mee shoved the pole that Wilma was
carrying through the bundles. Then she
balanced the pole on one shoulder and
started down the hill.

They took turns carrying the fuel
home.

12

CHIP opened the kitchen door and took the bundles off the pole.

Wilma wondered why Tang looked unhappy even though she said she was glad Mee and Wilma had found so much fuel.

Mee showed Chip and Wilma where to put it to dry with the pile of husks behind the stove. Wilma heard the sound of angry voices from behind the door to the living room.

"Willy," Chip whispered, "something must be wrong! Three old men have been talking to Chun for hours."

Ying was trying to read a book at the kitchen table. "They're the village Elders. Everybody has to obey them."

When Heing came home from school, he sat down at the table to do his lessons.

At last Chun opened the living room

door. "The Elders wish to speak to everybody in the house," he said. "Please come in here."

Tang was very pale. She took Heing and Mee into the living room. Ying followed with Wilma and Chip.

Three very old men sat at the table. Chun stood facing them.

The oldest of the three started to speak in a cracked and trembling voice. "You all know that custom forbids any stranger to come into our houses and eat and sleep with us. Chun has broken this rule, which has protected all of us for thousands of years. Now the entire village will be cursed with bad luck. We cannot allow people who break the ancient customs to live here."

Tang started to cry softly. Chun bowed his head, but Ying said, "Honorable Elders, please may I speak?"

The old men stared at him. Then the

oldest said, "Tell us what you wish to let us know."

Ying held his head high. "My father is not to blame. I met these children on Crag Island yesterday just as it was getting dark. They were lost and didn't know how to return home. I knew the village rule, but I begged my father to let them into our house, and he did not want to be unkind to two young people from a strange land."

"We are not unkind," the Elder said. "When strangers come, they can be fed and housed in the schoolhouse."

"That was all locked up for the night," Ying reminded him.

The Elders glared at him. Then they spoke to each other for a few minutes.

"Chun," the chief Elder said, "we have found the way to remove the curse from the village. Since it was your son's fault, he must leave the village tomorrow and take the two strange children away with him. You and the rest of your family may stay and farm your land as long as you keep to the rules."

All three Elders stood up, bowed stiffly, and went out by the living room door to the street.

Tang threw her arms around Ying and sobbed, and Chun buried his face in his hands.

13

TANG was too sad at the thought of Ying going away to do more than steam a pan of rice for supper.

"Don't feel bad, Willy. This wasn't your fault," Mee whispered. "And this is all we usually eat. We only get other things on special days."

"Having you here was special for me," Heing told Chip. "Ying never has time for anything but his books."

"I'm going to miss you, Willy," Mee said.

"So will I." Tang gave Wilma a hug. "You've been like a second daughter to me."

Wilma didn't know what to say. Up to

now, she and Chip had pretty much been having fun. Now they knew why Chun had looked scared when he met them.

Next morning, as soon as everyone had eaten a bowl of rice porridge, Tang rolled a big square of mosquito netting and a red blanket together in a strong mat of woven fiber. She brought out a large basket with a lid and two handles. Into the basket Tang put a bamboo stick, a piece of broken pottery, a brass basin, and a towel. She added a small round earthenware stove, some cooking pots, three bowls, six eating sticks, some wooden scoops, and a bag of rice.

Before Tang closed the lid of the basket, Ying stuffed in a padded jacket, a pair of pants, and shoes made of cotton cloth with felt soles. Then he put in his box of writing supplies and three books bound with wooden boards.

Mee handed Ying a leather bottle of boiled water to hang from his waist.

"You'll need some cash." Chun gave Ying a string of small round copper coins. Each coin had a square hole in the middle. "This is all I have. Most people when they're traveling loop these strings over their shoulders, but I think you should keep them hidden, even though they are not of great value."

Ying thanked his father and tied the string of cash around his waist, under his baggy jacket.

"Remember to stay away from lonely places and strangers," Chun warned his son. "There are fierce bandits in the open country. They capture people to sell them as slaves."

"Don't worry. We'll be careful," Ying promised.

Tang slipped a long pole through the handles on the basket. Two people, walking one behind the other, could each rest the pole on one shoulder and together carry the basket.

Wilma was taller than Chip. She and Ying decided to carry the basket and let Chip handle the bedroll.

Ying's mother and father hugged him. So did Mee and Heing. They all bowed to Chip and Wilma, who bowed in return. Then the three travelers left on their journey.

14

YING led the way back down the hill
they had climbed to reach his village. A
light rain was falling. The lake was covered with a heavy fog. It was so early in
the day that they met no one.

They waded to the little marshy island
and crossed the arched bridge to Crag
Island.

Ying took them up the cliff. It was hard
to climb with all they were carrying.
They passed the little summer house and
followed the ledge around the island.

The fog had risen from the lake. Far
below they could see a bridge standing
on wooden stilts high above the water.

Ying led them down a trail to the

bridge. There they put their loads on the ground.

"There's a boat in the water," Chip said.

"Stay here and guard the supplies," Ying said. He climbed down the huge rock that supported one end of the bridge.

Chip and Wilma saw the boatman row over to talk to him.

Suddenly a big black bird splashed out of the water with a fish in its beak. It dropped the fish into the boat. Then it perched on the rim of the boat and spread its wings to let them dry.

Several birds were on the rim of the boat. Three of them flew into the air and soared over the lake. They dived under the water. One returned with a small fish, which it gulped down.

When the other birds came back, they brought large fish and dropped them into the boat.

Wilma counted ten birds. "Why do they eat the little fish and drop the big ones into the boat?" she asked.

"Can't you see that they're wearing collars?" Chip said. "They *can't* swallow the big fish."

Ying finished talking to the boatman. He climbed back up the rock. "He'll take us across to a town on the mainland when he has enough fish to sell."

Ying worked with Wilma and Chip to lower the basket to the edge of the lake. Then Ying carried down the bedroll.

The boatman rowed as close to the rocks as he could. The children waded to the boat with their heavy load.

"This is Chip, and this is Willy," Ying

told the boatman. "And this is Moy," he said to Wilma and Chip.

The boatman smiled at them.

A curved canopy covered the rear of the boat. Moy helped his passengers stow their gear under it.

"Is Moy an old friend of yours, Ying?" Chip asked.

Ying grinned. "I just met him. He's a nice man. He's going to show me how to row this boat." Ying went to take hold of an oar.

15

MOY showed Ying how to row the boat. Chip and Wilma already knew how. Together they rowed for a while. The rain stopped, and the sun came out from behind the clouds.

The boatman had given each bird a name. "I raised them from chicks and trained them to fish for me," he said. "My father taught me the trade."

The bird Moy called Ding perched on his shoulder as they floated along.

Moy steered the boat across the lake and followed a canal through flooded rice fields to houses built right at the edge of the water. He anchored his boat among many others at the foot of a stairway. "This is where I sell my fish."

Ying thanked the boatman for the voyage. He took out his string of cash to pay him.

Moy shook his head. "Put your money away, Ying. I make money by selling fish. I *liked* having you and your friends for company."

People who wanted to buy fish were hurrying down the steps.

Chip and Wilma thanked Moy and said good-bye.

All three picked up the basket and the bedroll and made their way up the steep stairs to the street.

Shops along the narrow crowded street sold everything from used clothing to singing birds and beautiful lacquered bowls. Traders who had no shops piled their goods on stone slabs along the street. And roaming peddlers called out that they had fruit and fish and ducks for sale.

Wilma and Chip followed Ying through the crowd. Ying looked at the sun to be sure he was going in the right direction and didn't stop until they reached the edge of the town.

The sun was hot. When they had left the last house behind, they set down the basket and the bedroll in the shadow of a hill with trees growing on it.

Ying untied the leather water bottle from his waist. They each took a drink. Then they opened the basket. All of them were hungry.

"We should have brought fuel," Ying said.

Wilma looked through the field glasses and saw some dry grass and fallen branches near the top of the hill. "Come on, Chip," she said.

Together Wilma and Chip found enough fuel to cook the rice.

Ying took the piece of broken pottery out of the basket and whacked it against the bamboo stick. This caused a spark to fly into the dry grass and start it burning.

Chip decided to look through the glasses. "I think I see a spring near those trees."

Chip and Wilma each grabbed a cooking pot and went to fill them. They brought back water to boil on the stove.

The stove was just big enough for one pot. Ying put a pan of rice to steam over a pot of water.

While they were waiting for the rice to cook, Ying told Wilma and Chip his plans for the journey.

16

"I want to go to the Capital City," Ying told Chip and Wilma. "Many poets and artists and scholars live there. I need to study with someone who can teach me what I have to know to help govern the country.

"We'd better travel close to the water, so as not to get lost," Ying said. "There are woods around here, so we have to watch out for bandits."

"What do the bandits look like?" Chip asked.

"Wild and fierce," Ying answered,

"dressed in rags or almost naked. I've never seen one, but people have told me about them."

The rice was ready now, so Ying stopped talking and served it. They were all happy that Ying had cooked enough for second helpings.

Everybody felt better after the meal. Ying filled his leather bottle with boiled water. They cleaned the dishes and cooking pots and packed them back in the basket. Then they started off again.

Ying led them to the top of the hill. From here they could see the river winding through a rocky gorge. They kept as close to it as they could, but much of the time they were high above it, walking through woods or at the edge of cliffs.

When the sun began to be low in the sky, Wilma and the boys built another fire and cooked more of the rice for supper.

They were in a woods near the cliff that towered over the river. It seemed a good place to spend the night.

Just before dark Ying unrolled the fiber mat and spread it on the ground. He laid the red blanket on top of the mat. Then he used slender branches to make a curved frame to hold the mosquito netting over it.

"Time for bed!" Ying held back a flap of the netting so that Wilma and Chip could crawl under it and lie down on the blanket. When they were settled, Ying crawled in, too, and closed the curtain of netting behind him.

All around them insects made chirping noises. Wilma heard an owl hoot. But she was much too tired to listen. She closed her eyes.

The next thing she knew, the sun woke her. Birds were chirping overhead. It was morning!

Chip and Ying were already up. They had built a fire, and Ying had put a pan of rice porridge on the little stove.

Wilma crawled out from under the mosquito netting. She stood up and stretched.

She remembered seeing a little stream yesterday. Wilma decided to go and wash her face.

She followed a faint path through the woods. Just before she came to the stream, she heard the sound of rough voices.

17

WILMA stepped off the path and crawled through the underbrush. She peeked through a tangle of green leaves.

Four men wearing raggedy loincloths were down on their knees beside the stream. They were scooping up water and drinking out of their hands. Wilma saw that they all had long knives and fierce wild faces.

One of the men got to his feet. He looked taller and stronger than the others and seemed to be the leader. "Hurry up!" he snarled. "I can smell something cooking. Maybe we can share the meal." He gave a nasty laugh.

Wilma crawled to the path and ran back to where Chip and Ying were getting breakfast ready. She put her finger to her lips and whispered, "Bandits! They smelled the porridge cooking and are headed this way. We have to get out of here."

Ying grabbed his jacket and one book from the basket. They left everything else behind and silently made their way out of the woods to the top of the cliff.

It was very early in the morning. No boats were moving on the river below the cliff. Chip pointed to a path that led down to the water. "Let's go see what it's like down there."

"Maybe the path goes alongside the water," Wilma said.

Ying started down the path. Chip and Wilma followed him.

They walked quietly, trying not to start any stones rolling down and not talking to each other. The path twisted and turned, going around big rocks and over small ones.

At the bottom they came to a narrow stony beach. They walked along the edge of the water for about a mile.

A pile of black feathers was flopping around on the beach. Chip ran to see what it was. He picked up a black bird with a red collar. The bird's feet were tied together. Its wings were roped to its sides.

Chip took the bird over to show Ying and Wilma. "This looks like Ding," he

whispered. "Something must have happened to Moy!"

Ying pulled a knife from under his baggy jacket and cut the rope that bound the bird.

Chip stroked the bird's head. "Ding," he said softly. The bird turned his head to look at Chip. Then Chip held out his arm so that Ding stood on his outstretched palm.

"Where is Moy?" Chip asked.

Ding stretched his wings twice and flew up into the air. He circled the beach and then swooped down to land on a mound of freshly cut branches.

Chip ran after him. Wilma and Ying followed close behind.

When they reached the mound, all three began to lift off the branches. Right under the leafy cover, they found a boat like the one they had traveled in the day before.

As soon as they had uncovered the cloth canopy at the rear of the boat, the bird hopped down and looked under it.

Chip jumped into the boat and looked under the canopy, too. He made a sign to Ying to get out his knife.

Under the canopy Wilma and the boys saw a man who had been blindfolded and gagged. His hands and feet were tied with the same sort of rope that had bound the bird.

Ying cut the rope, but the man didn't move. And when Chip took the gag out of his mouth, he made no sound.

Wilma gently removed the blindfold. Now they could see that it really was Moy. But his eyes were closed.

"Ying!" Chip whispered. "Do you think he's dead?"

18

AT the sound of Chip's voice, Moy opened his eyes. He stared at the three young people. Then he put his finger to his lips and whispered, "Go away at once! The bandits will come to get me at any moment. If you're here, they'll capture you, too."

Ying put his book into the boat. Then he began to take off the rest of the branches and said, "We have to get this into the water."

Wilma and Chip helped him.

"There isn't enough time. Save yourself!" Moy said. But he, too, started to pull off branches.

Ding perched on Moy's shoulder while he worked. The bird stayed there when Moy and the others began to push the boat across the stony beach.

The boat was much heavier than it looked. Now and then they had to stop and roll some of the bigger stones out of the way.

Just as they had almost reached the water, Ding flew up into the air with a warning scream.

Wilma looked through the field glasses. Far down the beach she saw the four men from the woods coming around a bend of the cliff. "The bandits are coming!"

Moy gave a mighty shove. Wilma and the two boys pushed as hard as they could.

Slowly the boat slid into the river. Moy held on to it while the others climbed in. Then he pushed it into deep water and swam after it.

Ying helped Moy climb into the boat. The two of them took the oars and began to row.

The bandits were racing down the beach. When they reached the place where they had left Moy's boat, it was far out in the middle of the river and moving swiftly downstream.

Ding was perched on his master's shoulder. When they saw the boat in the water, Moy's nine other fishing birds flew down from the cliff to sit on the rim of the boat.

"The birds flew away when the bandits captured me," Moy said. "Ding stayed with me. The bandits were going to sell him. Fishing birds are valuable."

"Why did you come here?" Ying asked.

"While I was selling my fish yesterday, I heard someone talking about the good fishing on this stretch of the river. I know nobody ever seems to fish here. Since I live in my boat, I thought I'd come here to try my luck." Moy grinned. "My luck wasn't too good until you three showed up."

19

"I think *we* are lucky to have found *you*, Moy," Wilma told him. "The bandits were after us, and we couldn't have escaped them without your help."

"What happened to all that gear you young people were carrying yesterday?" Moy asked.

Ying showed him his book. "I saved this. We left everything else in the woods when Willy saw the bandits heading for our camp."

Moy's birds were all flying out over the river and coming back with fish, which they dropped into the boat.

"It *is* a good fishing place," Chip said.

"I had a boatful of fish when the bandits swam out and captured me. It was getting dark, and I didn't see them coming," Moy said.

"They gagged and bound me and tied up Ding. Then they rowed the boat to shore and dragged it onto the beach.

"The bandits stole the fish I'd caught and everything else I had. They covered the boat with branches. I spent the night in the boat. They left Ding on the beach because he kept biting them.

"I decided to pretend to be dead, so the bandits wouldn't take me away with them." Moy laughed. "Well, now I know why nobody wants to fish here."

All four were soaked to the skin and very hungry. Moy and Ying kept on rowing. When they were tired, Wilma and Chip took their turn at the oars. They wanted to get as far from the bandit coast as they could. The birds kept diving after fish and dropping the big ones into the bottom of the boat.

As the sun rose higher, their clothes began to dry. At last they came to a waterfront town. Moy tied his boat to a pier. The fish were flopping around in the boat.

Moy climbed out onto the dock. "Hand me the biggest fish, Ying."

Ying reached for a fish, but it slipped out of his hands. Chip grabbed it. Together the two boys lifted the fish to where Moy could take hold of it.

The boatman held it up. "Come and buy a fish so fresh, I can hardly hold on to it," he yelled.

A crowd began to gather. The big fish was sold to a woman who dropped it into a basket with a lid on it.

Ying and Chip were kept busy grabbing the fish and handing them to Moy.

Wilma wanted to help, but she dropped the fish as soon as they began to wiggle.

Soon Moy had sold all the fish. He climbed back into the boat. Ying helped him string the copper coins he had received.

"We should have kept one of the fish to eat ourselves," Moy said. "Oh, I forgot. I don't have anything to start a fire going."

He looked at the strings of coins and smiled. "But at least we have cash. Watch my boat for me. I'll be back soon."

Moy stepped out of the boat. He walked across the dock and into the town.

20

Moy returned in half an hour. He had bought a bag of rice, a pan, a dish, and a little stove like the one Ying had left in the woods. Moy held up a bamboo stick and a broken piece of pottery. "The man who sold me the stove gave me these," he said. "Now we can make a fire."

"We need fuel," Wilma reminded him.

"We'll have to go look for it," Moy said. He untied the boat and began to row. "Let's try the other side of the river. There's not much chance of finding any close to the town."

Wilma looked through the field glasses at the brown hills. She showed Moy a patch of reeds at the water's edge.

Moy rowed over to it, and Ying cut the reeds with his knife. Wilma and Chip spread them out to dry on the bottom of the boat. They had to find a place where there were no wet fish flopping around. The birds were busy again.

Some of the reeds were old and dried quickly. Ying managed to make a little fire in the boat. He boiled water from the river to steam the rice.

They used stiff green reeds as eating sticks and all ate from the dish Moy had bought. Wilma was so hungry that her stomach hurt. The warm rice helped.

After the meal, they went on rowing. The birds kept fishing.

Late in the day, they came to a town at the riverside. Moy tied his boat to a dock and sold most of his fish.

Afterward, Chip was helping Moy string the copper coins. "Ow!" He stopped to slap his bare arm.

Moy jumped to his feet. "I'd better hurry before the market closes," Moy said. He took the strings of cash and rushed away.

There was no wind now, and the mosquitoes began to gather. Wilma and Chip slapped at them, but they were bitten anyway. Ying was luckier since he was wearing his jacket with long sleeves.

When Moy returned, he carried a roll of mosquito netting and some sticks of pressed powder. "I didn't have enough cash for a mat and blankets," he said. "But this is more important. I had to pay a high price because only one stall in the market was still open." He lit a stick of pressed powder to keep the mosquitoes away from the boat.

A watchman was guarding the dock. So many boats were tied up here that it seemed like a street of houseboats. Moy thought it was safer to spend the night at the dock than to anchor in the river.

Ying steamed the rice, and Moy cooked a big fish until it was crisp and brown.

After supper, Moy propped up the oars to make a tent of the mosquito netting. Then all four of them lay down side by side under the netting on the hard boards of the boat.

The big birds perched on the rim of the boat with their heads tucked under their wings.

21

NEXT morning, as soon as they'd all shared a dish of rice, Moy untied his boat and rowed to the middle of the river. Ding perched on his shoulder, and Moy stroked the bird's head.

"Where are we going, Moy?" Ying asked.

"Wherever you like," the boatman answered. "You saved me from the bandits. The least I can do is help you get where you want to go."

"We want to go to the Capital City," Ying told him, "where I can really study to be a scholar."

"I'll take you there," Moy promised. After that, he didn't steer the boat into any of the canals, but stayed on the river. Whenever the birds had caught enough fish, Moy would dock at a town where he could sell them and buy things he needed.

As soon as he had enough money, Moy bought a pottery bowl and a china scoop for each of them so they could eat rice porridge first thing in the morning.

Rainy days were good for fishing, but when there was a fog, the birds just stayed on the boat. Some days the fish the birds caught were so small that the birds ate all of them. On those days, Moy didn't go shopping.

When he did shop, Moy always looked for bargains. He bought a secondhand quilt that was large enough for all of them to sleep on, and secondhand jackets that would fit Wilma and Chip. The jackets buttoned under their arms and felt strange, but they were warm. Nights on the river were damp and cold.

One day Moy came back to the boat

with a big smile on his face. "Look what I found in the market!" He handed Ying a roll of paper, a pointed brush, a stick of lampblack, and a mixing stone.

Ying was so happy, he couldn't thank Moy enough. "How did you know how much I wanted this?"

"This was what my cousin Trinh liked best when he was your age," Moy said. "He was just like you — always had his nose in a book. He lives in the Capital City now. Maybe he can help you." Moy turned to Chip and Wilma. "What are you two looking for in the Capital?"

The two children didn't know what to tell him.

Ying answered for them. "Chip and Willy think they were brought to our country by that toy Willy carries around her neck. They say they need magic to make it take them home again. Of course I don't believe in magic, but I've heard there are wise men in the Capital who do."

"It is a wonderful toy," Moy said. "I wouldn't be surprised at anything it would do."

Moy untied the boat from the dock and picked up an oar. Ding flapped over to sit on his shoulder until he spied a fish in the water.

Ying tucked the roll of paper and the other writing things into a corner under the canopy and went to help with the rowing.

When Ying and Moy were tired, Wilma and Chip took their turn at the oars.

22

For many days they traveled down the river. The towns were closer together now. The water began to be crowded with boats of all shapes and sizes. Many boatmen had their families with them.

One sunny morning, right after breakfast, Wilma looked at a boat anchored nearby. A woman in the boat was washing and hanging up clothes. "That's what we ought to do, Chip," she said.

"Don't be silly," her brother told her. "You can't get dirty on a boat!"

Wilma and Chip watched a small boy playing near the woman who was busy with her laundry. Suddenly the boy leaned over the rim of the boat and tumbled into the water.

Chip didn't waste a minute. He jumped into the river and swam to the rescue. The little boy tried to push Chip away.

Wilma pulled off her sneakers, dived overboard, and went to help.

The boy wiggled away from Chip.

Wilma tried to grab him to keep his

head out of the water. "I can't get a grip on this kid," she gasped.

Then Wilma and Chip heard the sound of laughter.

They looked up to see Moy looking down at them from his boat. He was laughing so hard, he couldn't speak. Ying came to see what was going on. He started to grin.

Chip was trying to untangle his foot from a rope that dangled from the boat where the woman was still washing her laundry. "What's the matter with all of you? Doesn't anyone care if we all drown?"

Moy stopped laughing. "Let go of the child," he said. "His mother will pull him into the boat when she has time."

Wilma took her hands off the little boy. He bobbed up and down in the water.

"He's tied to a little barrel," Ying explained, "so he's safe if he falls overboard."

Now Chip laughed. "I guess he does it all the time. He seems to like the water. Well, so do I!" Chip took off one of his sneakers. Now he could pull his foot free from the rope.

"Hand me both of your shoes, Chip." Moy reached down to take them from him.

Wilma started swimming. "Bet I can beat you to the end of the dock," she yelled to her brother.

Chip splashed after her.

By the time they got near the dock, the water was full of laughing children of all ages. They all thought it was a great idea to go swimming on a day like this.

"Willy," Chip said. "This is even better than Coney Island."

23

WHEN Chip and Wilma climbed back into the boat after their swim, their clothes were so wet and soggy that they changed into the baggy jackets Moy had given them.

Moy had just come back from the market with a wooden washtub with smooth stones in it. He filled it with water from the river.

While Ying and Moy rowed the boat and the birds fished, Wilma and Chip set to work to scrub their clothes.

There was no soap, but rubbing the clothes against the stones knocked the dirt loose. When the clothes were as

clean as they could get them, the two children spread them on the canopy.

The sun was hot. Before long, their clothes were dry. Chip and Wilma put them back on and went to take their turn at the oars.

The birds were busy fishing. Moy looked at what they had caught. "These aren't nearly as big as the ones that came from the bandit coast," he said. "But I don't think I'll fish there anymore. How about you, Ding?"

The bird flapped over to perch on Moy's shoulder and have his head scratched.

Ying sat in the shade of the canopy. He took out his brush and paper and began to write.

"Do you think we'll ever see Mom and Dad again, Willy?" Chip asked.

"Of course we will," Wilma told him. "Don't forget, we still have the field glasses!"

"Let me have the glasses, Willy." Chip reached for them.

Wilma handed them to him.

The river was getting much wider. After a while it became a large basin. Ahead of them the basin opened into a bay.

Chip was looking through the field glasses at the shoreline. "Willy, I think I see a *castle* over there!"

WILMA took the field glasses. She looked across the water.

At the foot of a beautiful row of hills she saw a thick stone wall with battlements along the top. Great square towers were placed here and there along the wall.

Wilma called to Moy. "What's that big castle over there?"

Moy shaded his eyes and tried to see

across the glittering water. Wilma went to hand him the field glasses.

Moy looked through them. "That's not a castle, Willy. It's the Capital City!"

He took charge of the oars. "These are dangerous waters. We don't want to be swept into the bay. The tides there sometimes roll in with waves as tall as a house."

Ying was very excited. He took turns with Chip and Wilma to look through the field glasses. As they got closer, they saw that the great wall surrounded a city. The square towers were gates.

Moy steered the boat toward a crowded pier, looking for a place to dock near one of the big city gates.

Just when they all thought they'd have to row to a spot much farther from the gate, a boatman pulled up his anchor and started upstream. Moy tied up his boat in the space that was left empty.

The birds hadn't caught as many fish or fish as large as they had caught in places where there were fewer fishermen, but the fish here were so fresh that they were still alive and trying to jump out of the boat.

Moy saw that most people were buying fish at the market stalls set up just outside the city gate. He grabbed a fish in each hand and climbed onto the dock. "Fresh-caught fish!" he yelled at the top of his voice.

A woman with a market basket came to see. She bought both fish Moy was holding. "Look at these," she told a friend. The friend decided to buy some of Moy's fish, too.

Moy sold the fish as fast as Ying and Chip could hand them to him. Very soon they were all gone.

Moy got a better price for them than he'd expected.

After Ying helped him string the copper coins, Moy went to talk to the watchman who guarded the dock.

He came back to tell Ying, Chip, and Wilma, "The watchman has promised to make sure that the boat is safe while we're gone. It's early enough for me to take all three of you to look at the sights of the city. Tomorrow I'll go with Ying to see my cousin, and Chip and Willy can watch the boat."

In the nearby marketplace, Moy bought a long blue robe such as many men wore here in the Capital. He tucked the robe in at his ankles. Then he led the way through the enormous arched gate in the thick city walls.

25

THE city seemed to be courtyards within courtyards. Peeping through a gate, Wilma and Chip saw houses with tile roofs that curved up at the edges and stuck out far beyond the walls.

Chip pointed to the part-bird, part-fish creatures carved at each end of the high, ridged posts in the center of the rooftops. "What are those for?"

"Those are charms to protect the houses against fire and other dangers," Moy told him.

Most of the houses were orange-red with gray roof tiles. But there were also palaces with deep blue or yellow roof tiles, and flowery designs painted on the walls just below the roofs.

Wilma saw that all the courtyards had gardens.

Some of the streets were crossed by triple arches. The important shops had false fronts, with masts and crossbeams and little fake roofs.

When they passed the busy inns and teahouses, the delicious smells from them made all four travelers very hungry. Moy bought rice cakes from one street vendor, and kumquats from another. They ate them on the street.

"Where is the Western Lake that people talk so much about?" Ying asked.

"That's outside the city wall," Moy said.

They walked to the west of the city. On the other side of the big gate they came to the lake. It was at the foot of high, tree-covered hills.

Each of them took a turn looking through the field glasses at the brightly painted boats sailing there. With the glasses they could also make out fine houses and beautiful temples built along the shores and on the little islands in the lake.

Moy looked at the sun. "It's getting late." Wilma hung the glasses around her neck, and they all went back into the city.

Moy took them into a big shed to see people weaving silk on wooden looms. A little later, Ying made Chip and Wilma stop to look into a shop where men printed books on thin paper with wood blocks.

Suddenly four strong men came down the crowded street carrying a carved box with doors and windows and a curly roof. The men shoved everybody out of the way to make room for the fancy box.

"There's a fine lady in there," Moy whispered.

Wilma was caught in the crush of people. She was separated from Chip and

their friends. It was getting dark.

"Chip!" Wilma called.

A moment later she heard her brother answer, "Willy, where are you?"

Then she heard Moy's fish-selling bellow: "Stay where you are, Willy! We'll find you."

26

Moy made his way through the crowd to where Wilma was standing. Chip and Ying were close behind him.

"We'd better all hold hands," Moy said. He took hold of one of Wilma's hands, and Chip took the other.

Ying grabbed Chip's other hand. The four of them held tight to each other until the crowd scattered.

Shopkeepers were lighting round paper lanterns with signs written on them. The lanterns glowed in the dark shadows.

By the time Moy had found the way to the gate near the dock, the moon was in the sky. The watchman had a lantern.

He helped Moy find his boat among the many tied to the dock. Moy paid him for keeping an eye on the boat while they were away.

The fishing birds were already asleep on the rim of the boat.

Chip and Wilma helped Ying get a fire going. He boiled water and steamed a big pan of rice. As soon as they had finished eating, they all lay down on the quilt under the mosquito netting and fell fast asleep.

In the morning, after they'd finished their porridge, Ying and Moy started to get ready to visit Moy's cousin. Moy put on his new blue robe.

Ying washed his face and hands. He whacked his baggy pants and jacket to knock off the dirt. "I should have washed them when you washed your clothes, Willy. But I didn't know we were going to be in the Capital City so soon."

"You look fine, Ying." Moy climbed onto the dock. "Come along."

Ying left the boat and followed Moy to the city gate.

The birds had been flying out over the water since the first light of day. Most of what they caught was so small that they could swallow it, but Ding finally came back with a fairly large fish. He dumped it into the boat and flew over to perch on Chip's shoulder.

Chip rubbed the bird's long neck.

Ding stretched his wings and held them out to dry.

Chip laughed. "Willy, look at Ding. Doesn't he make you want to tickle him?"

Wilma didn't answer. She picked up the quilt, shook it, and then folded it up again. Next she looked through all the things under the canopy. She even opened up the bag of rice. After that, Wilma began to search every inch of the boat.

Chip was surprised to see her pick up the flopping fish to make sure there was nothing under it. "What are you looking for, Willy?"

"The field glasses," Wilma said in a very small voice. "I haven't seen them since yesterday."

27

CHIP sat quite still with the big bird on his shoulder. He just looked at Wilma and didn't speak.

"I know I had the glasses when we left the Western Lake," Wilma said. "But after that, I don't remember using them. I thought they were around my neck. I didn't miss them till just now."

"Willy," Chip said, "they must have been pulled off in that crowd we were caught in."

"I would have felt that," Wilma told him.

Chip stood up. Ding hopped onto the rim of the boat. The two children went on looking for the field glasses.

"We ought to go back into the city and

look everywhere we walked after we left the lake," Chip said.

"We have to watch the boat for Moy," Wilma reminded him.

Neither of them said what they both knew — that now there was no chance of their returning home. It seemed a long time before Moy and Ying came back.

"My cousin wanted us to dine with him, Willy," Moy said, "but when I told him about you and Chip, he said he would send a servant tomorrow to watch the boat. We can all have the midday meal with him tomorrow."

Ying's eyes were shining. "Moy's cousin Trinh said he would take me to the National Academy. The scholars there will tell me what to study to work for the government."

When Wilma and Chip told them that the field glasses were missing, both Ying and Moy agreed with Chip that they had been lost when Wilma was trapped in the crowd.

"There's no use going to look for the glasses in the city, Willy," Moy said. "The thief must have cut the cord that held them with a knife. You're lucky you weren't hurt!"

"Why would anyone want to steal them?" Wilma argued. "Nobody here knows what they're good for." She was close to tears.

"Some people are so poor, they steal anything," Moy said.

"Chip and Willy think the glasses are the only thing that can take them home again," Ying told him.

Moy put his arms around the two children. "I'll be happy to take care of you," he promised.

Ying took out the writing things Moy had given him and set to work.

"Is this another poem?" Wilma asked.

"I'm writing to my family," Ying told
her. "They'll be glad to know we're all
right."

Moy sold most of the few fish his birds
had caught. He saved two of them to
cook for supper and serve with the rice.

Wilma and Chip tried to be cheerful
and pretend they'd forgotten about the
field glasses. But deep down inside, they
were both more unhappy than they had
ever known they could be.

28

THE next day, after his cousin's servant came to watch the boat, Moy led the three children through the big gate into the city. His cousin Trinh lived on a narrow street paved with stone.

The house was behind a gray-blue brick wall. Two stone steps as long as the house went up to a carved wooden door with a round red lantern on each side of it. Trinh's name was written in black on each lantern.

A smaller lantern was over the door. Two strips of red paper with good wishes written on them were pasted on each side of it.

Moy pulled a silken cord. Somewhere a bell tinkled.

A servant opened the door in the wall.
On the other side was a garden. The
servant led the way across a little bridge.

Wilma looked down into a pond with
water lilies and goldfish in it.

On the other side of the bridge they
came to an entrance hall and went into
the house. They followed the servant to
the room where Trinh was waiting to
welcome them.

Chip and Wilma liked him at once. He looked a lot like Moy. They were about the same size and both had laughing eyes and the same kind of friendly face.

Trinh was wearing a black skullcap and a long red robe with a golden dragon embroidered on the back.

Flowers made of seashells had been set into the carved black wood of the tables and benches in the room. There were large vases of red and gold. Pictures painted on rice paper or silk hung on the walls.

The pictures were all of high mountains, lakes or rivers, and mist. Wilma and Chip thought they looked a lot like the painting in their spare room.

"These are my friends, Chip and Willy," Moy told his cousin.

"I am honored by your visit," Trinh said and bowed to each of them in turn. "I hope you have a good appetite. My cook has been busy all morning with this meal." He took them into the next room, where a big round table had been set with places for five people.

They ate from thin china bowls with flowers painted on them and drank flower-scented tea from tiny cups. The sticks for eating were of polished ivory.

Dinner began with fruit and sweet pastries and ended with melon soup. In between there were bowls of snowy rice, platters of crispy fish baked whole, mushrooms of all shapes and sizes, roast pork, tender chicken slices, tiny ginkgo nuts, and many other delicious things.

For some time, everybody was too busy eating to talk. At last they all reached a point where they had to say they couldn't eat another bite.

Trinh smiled. "Perhaps this is a good time for Chip and Willy to tell me their story. Both Ying and Moy said it was a very strange one."

29

CHIP and Wilma started to tell their story. Ying and Moy continued it. Wilma finished by telling how the field glasses had been lost.

"What did the glasses look like?" Trinh asked her.

"They're hard to describe," Wilma said, "but maybe we could draw them."

"Please come with me." Trinh went back into the room with the beautiful furniture. His four guests followed him.

He stopped in front of one of the paintings. "Is this like the picture you have in your house?"

"All these pictures are sort of like it," Chip said, "but ours has a lake, and this has a waterfall."

"Did the same person paint all of them?" Wilma asked.

"No, all artists here paint in this way. It is the custom," Trinh told her. He opened a door and led them all through the garden to another building. "This is my workshop."

There were shelves full of books and rolls of paper. On a clean desk lay brushes and sticks of colored ink, along with a half-finished watercolor painting. The painting showed a lake at the foot of high wooded hills.

"That looks like the Western Lake," Wilma said, "but you can't see it from here. How can you paint it?"

"In our country, we paint what we remember." Trinh rolled up the painting and put it on a shelf. He laid a piece of paper on his worktable, dipped a brush into a cup of water, and rubbed it on a stick of lampblack. "Who remembers

what the magic glasses looked like?"

Ying and Moy watched as Chip tried to draw the glasses. They explained to Trinh what the glasses looked like. Wilma drew on top of what Chip had drawn. At last, all four made circles with their fingers and held them to their eyes to show Trinh what they meant.

"This part is black metal," Wilma said, pointing to the drawing. "And these parts are glass. You look through here."

Trinh nodded. Then he spread a big sheet of paper on the desk. "Willy, do you and Chip remember what your home looks like?"

"I do," Chip said. "Our house is taller than yours. It has stone steps in front, and double doors with tall glass windows in them."

Trinh handed him the brush. "Draw it!"

"Willy draws better than I do." Chip gave her the brush. "There are five steps up to the stoop," he reminded her, "then another one right at the door. The doorknob on the right is shinier."

Wilma drew the steps. Trinh wanted to know what color they were. Wilma helped him mix the right reddish-brown. Then Trinh added shadows so the steps looked solid. Chip kept reminding Wilma of little details. Working together, they drew the front door.

The picture began to look so much like the home she would never see again that Wilma couldn't bear it. She dropped the brush and covered her face with her hands. "I can't go on."

"Willy," Trinh said softly. "You *must!*"

30

WILMA bit her lip to keep from crying. She put in a few brushstrokes to show the venetian blinds on the windows. Trinh added little touches of watercolor. Chip took the brush and drew an oblong window with the house number on it right over the doors.

"That picture looks so real, I feel as if I could walk up those steps," Moy said.

"Only *we* never will anymore!" Chip threw down the paintbrush. "I don't know why we had to do this to remind ourselves that we can't go home again."

"Maybe you can." Trinh lifted something off a shelf. "A poor man stopped me in the street this morning. I bought this from him not because I wanted it, but because he looked so hungry. I don't have a use for it, but maybe you and

Willy will find one." He handed Chip an old pair of field glasses.

The black paint was wearing off them, and the rim was missing from one lens. Someone had cut the shoelace that was tied to the glasses.

For a minute, Wilma and Chip couldn't say anything. Moy came over to give them each a hug.

Ying bowed. "If there *is* such a thing as magic, and you are leaving, I will miss you."

"We can never thank any of you enough," Wilma said.

Trinh pinned the painting to the wall of his study.

Chip turned the field glasses back to front. Wilma stood close beside him. She had to stoop a little because she was taller than her brother. They each looked through one of the large lenses at the picture they had painted.

At first it looked far, far away.

Then it came closer and closer until it filled the circle of light in front of them. Once again, Wilma found herself alone in a dark tunnel, but this time she didn't waste any time yelling for Chip. She ran and ran until at last she reached the end of the tunnel. She climbed down to the walk in front of her own front stoop.

Chip jumped out of the other tunnel. In a very few moments, both tunnels were gone.

The field glasses lay on the walk. Chip picked them up and raced up the steps. Wilma came after him and rang the doorbell.

Mrs. Gerston opened the door. "What a surprise! I thought you were upstairs," she said. "Well, I'm glad you didn't go any farther than this. It's time for supper."